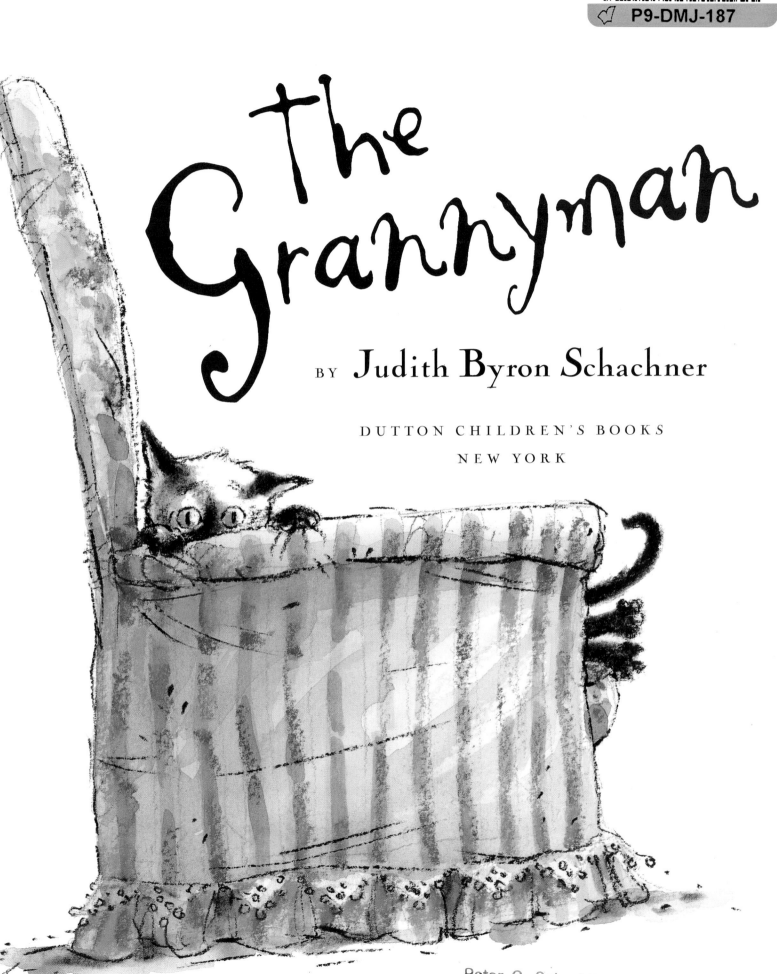

The Grannyman

BY Judith Byron Schachner

DUTTON CHILDREN'S BOOKS

NEW YORK

For...

Pete

Frankie

Mr. Mickey

Simon

Skippy

Boo Boo

Gooney

Birdy

Tink

Gibson

Babygirl

Library of Congress Cataloging-in-Publication Data
Schachner, Judith Byron.
The Grannyman/by Judith Byron Schachner. —1st ed.
p. cm.
Summary: Simon the cat is so old that most of his parts have stopped working,
but just when he is ready to breathe his last breath, his family brings home
a new kitten for him to raise.
ISBN 0-525-46122-1 (hardcover)
[1. Cats—Fiction. 2. Old age—Fiction.] I. Title
PZ7.S3286Gr 1999
[E]—dc21 98-52964 CIP AC

Published in the United States by Dutton Children's Books,
a division of Penguin Putnam Books for Young Readers
345 Hudson Street, New York, New York 10014
http://www.penguinputnam.com/yreaders/index.htm
Designed by Ellen M. Lucaire
Printed in Hong Kong
First Edition

7 9 10 8

Simon was a very old cat.

With the exception of his nose, most of his parts had stopped working long ago. He was blind and deaf, and his bones creaked as he climbed up and down the stairs.

Simon's family adored him and did all they could to keep him comfy in his old age.

Mealtimes were messy for their toothless old cat.
So the family bought Simon a bib to catch all the dribbles.
It's bad enough that I have to eat baby food, thought Simon,
without having to look like one, too.

But Simon loved the many heat treatments his family provided for him throughout the house. He basked and baked his achy bones until he was almost too hot to touch.

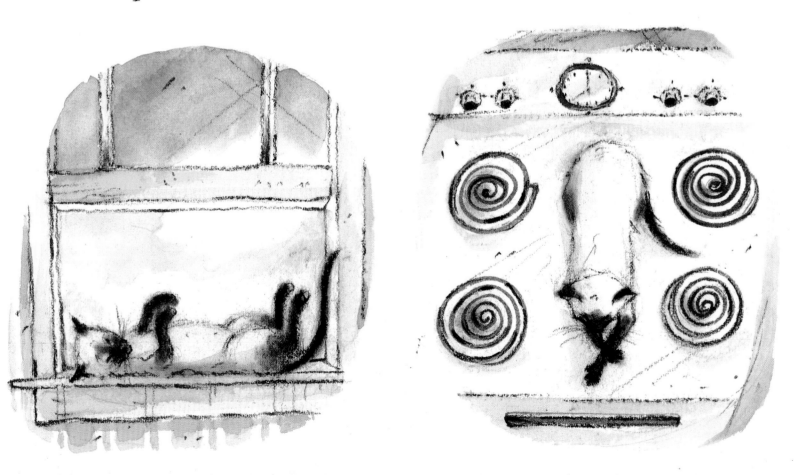

When Simon slept in bed at night, he snored and sneezed and drooled and breathed stinky old cat breath right into their faces, but his family didn't mind because they would do anything for their dear old cat.

On other nights he stayed put on the calico chair in the
corner, staring into space while he shuffled through a lifetime
of old memories.

Simon could still remember what it was like after he was born. The place was crawling with kittens that looked exactly like him.

One by one, each of the kittens went off to new homes with nice families. All but him. Nobody wanted the runt with the crooked tail and the runny nose.

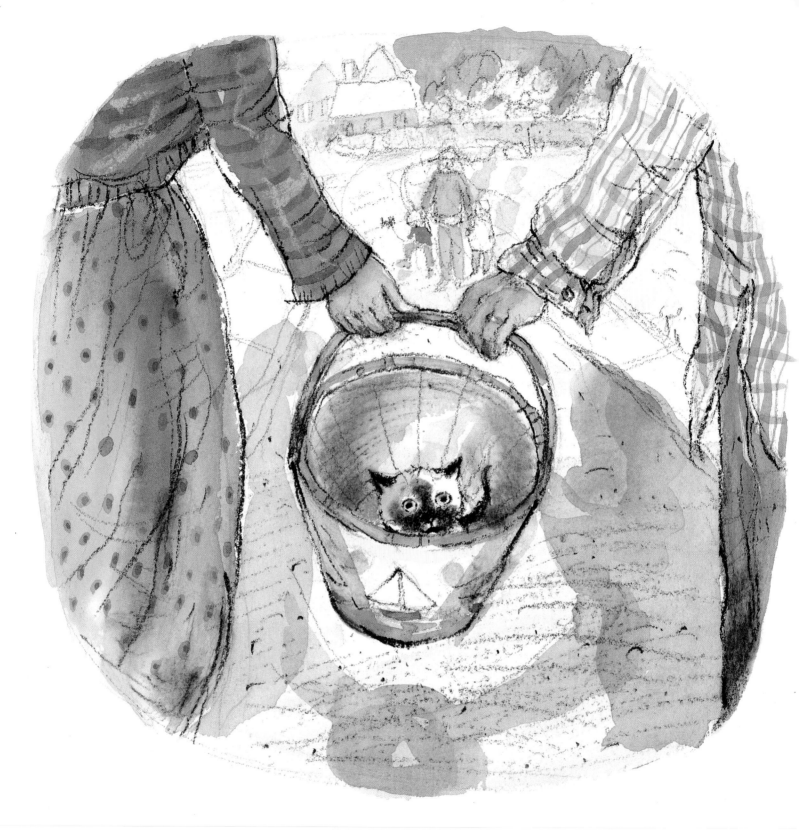

But then one day a nice couple found him irresistible, especially his crooked tail. They put a hankie to his nose, placed him in a bucket, and carried him to their home. They called him Simon.

Simon loved being a kitten. He climbed, he clawed,
he chased, and he chewed everything in sight.

Simon sculpted fluffy works of art out of several chairs and a chintz-covered couch. "Bad boy," cried the couple, and they clipped his claws. Simon's sculptures were never the same again.

The older Simon grew, the more he helped out around the house. He pruned the plants with his teeth . . .

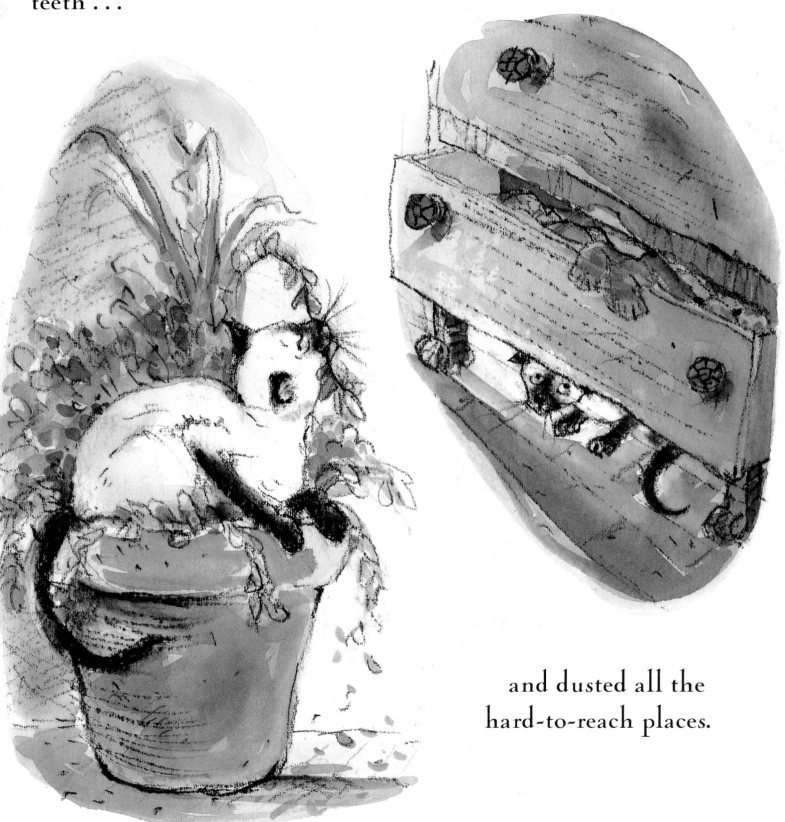

and dusted all the hard-to-reach places.

Simon's family grew in size, and so did his responsibilities.
Within three years, two new pets arrived, and Simon taught
them both how to be good cats.

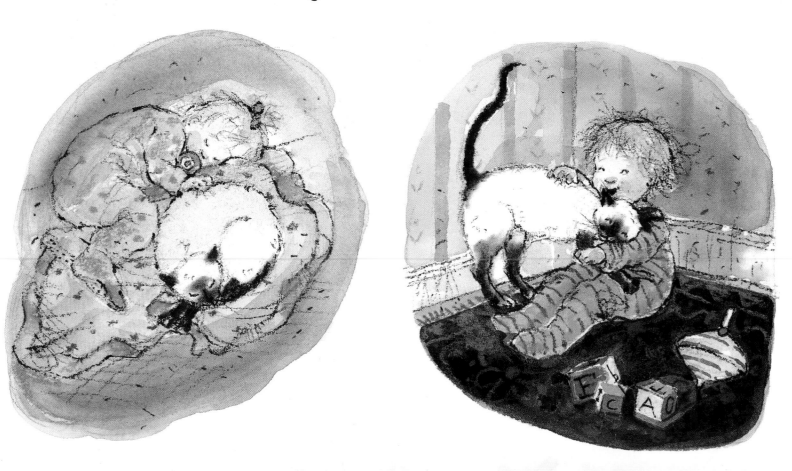

In his middle age, Simon acquired a taste for
classical music. He played Bach duets with his family
and performed an occasional solo at midnight.

Music always made Simon hungry, so he filled up on Kitty Krunchies in the kitchen. Then he hunted wildebeest with the great cats of the Serengeti.

Simon's life had been so full.

Full of mice,

full of hisses,

full of hugs,

and full of kisses.

But now things were different. Simon needed his family's help more than ever, and he felt their pity with every little pat on the head.

He felt so useless that at ten o'clock on a Tuesday night,
Simon stuck his bony old legs into the air and breathed his last.

Or so he thought—but then, in less than a minute, his family plopped something soft right on top of their old cat's tummy.

Simon sniffed to the left, and he sniffed to the right. Why, it's
a little kitten, thought Simon. Even though it had been years ago,
Simon remembered how he helped the other new pets when they
had come to the house. He wondered if he could still do it.

With great difficulty, Simon climbed down from his chair and carried the kitten downstairs to a fresh saucer of milk.

Then he demonstrated a whisker-washing. The kitten did his best to imitate the old cat.

When Simon twitched his tail, the kitten leaped onto his head, expecting to ride around the room.

A little while later, Simon led the kitten over to his box.
It took so long for the kitten to heap a mountain of litter onto
the floor that Simon decided to take a nap.

When Simon woke up, the kitten was gone. The old cat hobbled his way back up to the calico chair to sit alone in a sliver of moonlight. It must have been a dream.

Or so he thought.

Just then something soft and small jumped right on top of him. Simon sniffed to the left, and he sniffed to the right. Why, it's my kitten, thought Simon.

Simon began to give the kitten a bath. He washed his little ears and licked his little nose. He groomed his frisky tail and cleaned between each of his tiny toes. Then a grumbly-rumbly purr stirred deep within his chest, and he curled himself around his little pet.

When *Simon's* family saw how tenderly he cared for the new kitten, they loved him even more. *So* it was with the greatest respect that they gave their dear old cat a brand-new name.

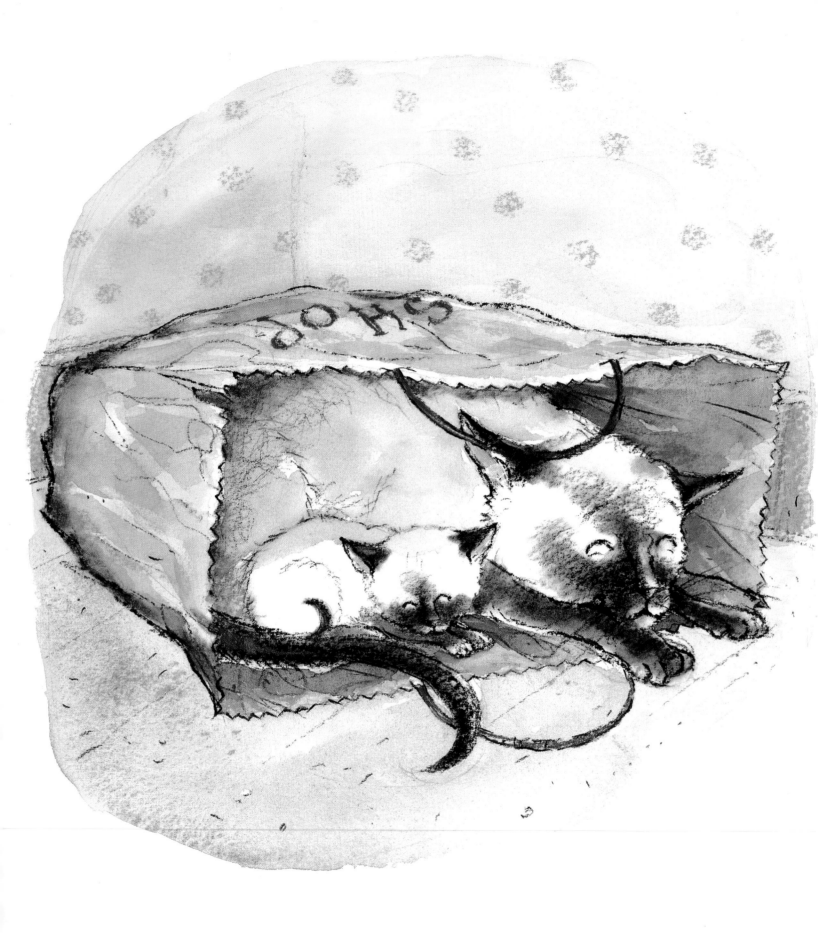

They called him the Grannyman.